The Nuclear Missile of Ellsw  T5-CAN-884
short stories

by Stan Strikolas   copywrite 2022

The Nuclear Missile of Ellsworth Street and other short stories

by Stan Strikolas

The nuclear missile of Ellsworth Street

The Apollo moon landings of 1970 filled the boys with an ambition to explore the sky above them. School had just ended, and the house at the end of Ellsworth Street would have four birthdays for four brothers. The inspiration for Rocketry would also permeate to parents as, at some point, one of the brothers got an Estes Rocket kit. The house on Ellsworth Street was an old Victorian-style balloon house at the end of the Street, built at the turn of the century with five bedrooms, a living room you could throw a football in, and 2 yards, one for football, one for Baseball. It bordered a fantastic universe for four brothers. On one side was the Hill going down to the Chuctanunda creek, an old creek that had been there long before the house was. Also, at the bottom of that Hill was a Dam made by early settlers to grind corn. The damn made the pond what was perfect for catching crayfish and sunfish. To the north side of the house going up, Clizbe Avenue Was old Mrs. Rezneak. She complained when they set off fireworks and called the cops. Luckily uncle Les (Officer Danfear) responded to the call. "Boys, you gotta set those fireworks off somewhere else; she'll just get annoyed and keep calling." To the northwest of the house was Morrello's, they had a great pool but no room to play, so they were naturally part of the Ellsworth street gang. Then going down the Street to McClary School were the Kryzacks and old Mrs. Osterhout. Mrs. Osterhout was the good old lady compared to Mrs. Rezneak, who was the mean old lady. Mrs. Osterhout gave the boys employment by paying two dollars to mow the lawn. The gang took turns doing it all summer. Two Dollars was a lot of money in 1970; two dollars could get you comic books, baseball cards, and maybe even a chance to play on the new pinball machine at Finley's store. That summer, a line was going out the door of kids waiting their turn to play the new pinball machine, the first of its kind in the neighborhood. Right next to McCleary elementary school, Finley's was the first they saw a pinball machine.

McClary's also had a long mowed front lawn perfect for playing football on. The Morrello's were joined by the Hansons, Marx, Schmitmans, and Ottati and Stankus would all congregate at the Ellsworth Street house with the four brothers as it was a large yard and centrally located tween McClary's, the Chuctanunda creek and Isabel's Baseball field. The Fourth of July was always a big holiday as lighting off

Roman candles and bottle rockets, Followed the Big fire in the fireplace. The boys called it "firecracker fever" this feeling can best be described as a combination of soda cans from Bev Pack, eating hamburgers under apple trees, watching sparklers, Roman candles pop in the sky and at the same time, seeing that endless amount of freedom in that same sky. Lazy summer evenings were spent playing hide and seek, followed by a big fire set in the fireplace by their dad.

One summer evening following a birthday, one of the boys got an Estes rocket kit. It was quickly set off in the yard of Ellsworth Street to the wonder of the whole gang as they kept looking up. Morrello's quickly followed then Ottati, leading to the Estes rockets and the inevitable space race on Ellsworth Street. The four brothers had set off their Estes rocket sooner than other neighborhood kids came by with their Estes rockets. The launchpad had to move, Mrs. Rezneak and her phone calls. So up to Isabel's field, the gang went with the inevitable question "who's got the highest Rocket?" who's got the Biggest Rocket? It was an excellent site to see a rocket go higher in the sky. It was highly contagious because setting off one rocket led to the desire to set off another.

Ellsworth Street house had an old retaining wall built with the house and looked as old as the house. It provided an excellent place for young brothers to play with Tonka Trucks. One day the two younger brothers were at the wall driving their toy trucks up and down the old wall when they stopped what they were doing.

A semi-truck pulled up, with their dad behind the wheel. It had a large load covered by canvas in the back. He told them to keep an eye on the truck as he went inside. Of course, this was too much of a temptation for the two boys: they could see parts of what was beneath the fabric, and the smaller one slipped inside to get a closer look. What he saw made him exclaim: "It's a big rocket! How can it be a rocket? It's too big!" The father had been working for the Scotia naval Depot today, making his rounds to Western New York transporting military supplies. As they later discovered, he'd stopped in with an intercontinental ballistic missile (without a warhead). All the boys realized it was the biggest Estes Rocket they'd ever seen.

That put Ellsworth Street ahead in the space race, which put Ellsworth Street ahead in the Estes rocket race, making Ellsworth Street the unchallenged local superpower.

Of course, being the unchallenged local superpower comes with grave responsibilities. Immediately, word got out, and within 15 minutes, half a dozen of the Ellsworth street gang was on the sidewalk looking at this massive big rocket. The whole gang was peeking under the canvas; Morrello's, Hansons, Marx, Schmitmans, Ottati, and Stankus knew this was a red-letter day. Ellsworth street had a nuclear missile. Intelligent life and military secrets are two oxymorons.

They began to make plans for how best to keep the nuclear missile a secret. Some suggested putting a guard on it every night, others wanted to create a clandestine communication system in case of an emergency. But most agreed that if word got out about the rocket, there would be chaos and panic in Ellsworth Street. So, they began to come up with ways to keep it quiet and safe. They decided on having a rotating guard duty amongst themselves and came up with different aliases in case anyone asked questions about who was guarding the missile. They also created a system of communication where they could quickly alert each other if something were to happen with the rocket or if someone asked questions about it. Finally, the gang set up measures for dealing with any outside force or government intervention that might try to take their nuclear missile away from them. With all these measures in place, there was no doubt that Ellsworth Street had become an area of true power and security. Even though they did not own an actual nuclear weapon, they certainly felt empowered by their ability to protect their neighborhood from outside forces and potential threats while keeping their secret safe.

Finally, the father's 30-minute lunch break was over, and he returned to his truck to deliver his load. As he drove away in his truck, the Ellsworth Street gang watched him leave with a feeling of sadness. The Estes not-so-secret nuclear missile was gone. Everyone wanted to know more about this mysterious nuclear missile on Ellsworth Street, but no one knew exactly what was going on there or how powerful it really was or even if it could be used as a weapon at all. Like a summer Thunder shower, it came, looked threatening, delivered a lot of rain and some wind, and passed away. After which a sunny summer day continued. The brothers continued to tinker with their go-kart and make more Estes rockets. Life in Ellsworth Street returned to normal. Summer continued, but the boys would never forget that one hour they had the nuclear missile on Ellsworth Street. They talked about it often while racing around in their go kart or launching rockets into the night sky.

Road trip 74

The four brothers grew up in one place from sunrise to sunset. Their country was Ellsworth Street, Clizbe Avenue, McClary School, Finley's market, Rockton Wye, Saint Casimir's church, and Isabel's field. If you grew up in this country, you would have the perception of being content, and you would grow up saying to yourself, this is your country. Candy the Collie was the family dog and was always there doing what shepherds did, herding the boys and ensuring they were always in one place. That is, of course, what shepherds do.

Often the father would take the four brothers to the thruway overpass entrance, park the car, sit there, and watch the trucks and cars go by on I-90. Semi-tractor trailers would pass, making that low hum diesel engine noise as they went under the thruway bridge. The boys would watch them until they went over the Hill and disappeared over the western horizon.

At McClary Elementary school, the teacher had a map on the wall. It's a map of the United States; there was a pin marking Amsterdam, New York. Beyond the pin were towns, rivers, lakes, mountains, valleys, cities, and roads, lots and lots of roads. The Eisenhower interstate highway system seemed to spread like veins in a body to the Pacific Ocean. The United

States seemed unimaginably large, but it was on a map on the wall. It was only a map, a piece of paper, not a country. The boys knew their country. In the summer of 1974, all this was going to change.

The mother spent the evening packing for the younger boys. The father did the final check of the tires, checked the oil for the AMC ambassador station wagon, and attached a tow hitch to the back to pull a small trailer for the extra luggage. The 1970s AMC ambassador replaced his 1960s Studebaker Lark Wagonaire. The father always supported the smaller car companies and would have used a Studebaker if the company didn't go under. The AMC has no air conditioning and will be transporting the mother, father, and six of their eight children. They're going to stop in Osceola, Iowa, to visit the second sister working there for the summer, then to the Pacific Coast & Disneyland. The oldest brother stays home and works. The mother will keep a diary and record the events for the next 15 days.

"Friday, June 21, 1974, prepared for trip; Candy spent our last day with us". When a family dog passes away, everyone is silent. The boy's natural Shepherd was old and had her last day on earth. She played with the young Brothers as a good shepherd does. Everyone goes to bed early in expectation of tomorrow's western journey.

"Saturday, June 22, 1974, started on our Western trip at 5:35 am". Soon the names of town and exits and houses and farms seemed to be rolling by at a fantastic rate. They stopped for lunch at Howard Johnson's in Erie, Pennsylvania, and for gas in Lagrange, Indiana, at 7:30 pm. The father didn't stop driving; he drove through most of the night, stopping for gas. For the father, the car was his instrument, and he played it with the precision of Chopin performing his nocturnal Op. all the boys could do was sit back and watch the cars on the highway.

"Sunday, June 23, 1974, arrive at Osceola Iowa 11:30 am." the family stopped for church services and then met the second sister at the R&R camp. The family stayed there for a night and a half.

"Tuesday, June 25, 1974, had a tour of the University of Iowa Ames." this is the college that the second sister and soon the first sister will be attending. They encounter for the first time those pragmatic Iowans, descendants of German farmers who settled in middle America without any fuss or fanfare but with only hard work and endurance.

"Wednesday, June 26, 1974, day of departure." The boys said goodbye to the two sisters. Going through the vast open landscape where the occasional small house or tree only disrupts corn, soybeans, and wheat fields. They had seen the signs all day that said: "Wall Drug 567 miles to go." the billboards started outside Chicago but seemed to be at every mile marker. The advertising worked. They stopped in Irene's motel in Wall, South Dakota, for the night.

"Thursday, June 27, 1974, drive through Badlands, Mount Rushmore." During a picnic lunch at mount Rushmore, the brothers ask their father why these men are on a mountain. "Because there are great Presidents," he replied. "We have to save our money for emergencies so will stop at campgrounds there are cheaper" father said. "I want to relax and unwind, and I want to stay at a hotel," the mother countered, this discussion would go on through the trip. After a day of sightseeing, the family stopped at the Sheridan Wyoming KOA campground. The boys, all accustomed to camping, enjoyed being outside in that western sky. "Watch out for the bears," the father said. There were no bears that night.

"Friday, June 28, 1974, Yellowstone national park."

if you are in a large family and your parents are not rich, you, like this family, are shown a snapshot of America. Yellowstone is on that short list of places that shout out loud. "This is America." The boys spend most of the day in Yellowstone and spend the night in a hotel in Afton, Wyoming, and the mother wins the debate that night.

"Saturday, June 29, 1974, Wyoming, Utah, Elko Nevada." The brothers floated in the Great Salt Lake and looked up at mountains higher than any they had seen back east. It was very hot but dry, with trees few and far between. The desert landscape takes shape. The family spends the night at the KOA campground.

"Sunday, June 30, 1974, Reno Nevada, across the Sierra Nevada Mountains to California." the family drives all day. At Reno, the father wins $25 on slots, then the big mountains climb took over an hour. The family goes higher until at the top, stopping at a pull-over to see the other side and California. They were stopping in Sacramento, California. The drive was a visual feast itself.

"Monday, July 1, 1974, leave Sacramento Ramada inn very nice two rooms air-conditioned, heated pool arrives in San Francisco at noon time walk around Fisherman's wharf."

"Tuesday, July 2, 1974, drive down Highway to Los Angeles", went on the beach early in the morning, saw the sunrise over the Pacific Ocean. Disneyland at 8:30 am, and crowds outside the park were already large. The day ended too soon as the boys could have gone on the rides forever. They spent the night in Ramada Inn of Riverside.

"Wednesday, July 3, 1974, left Riverside California at 9:00 am, arrived in Las Vegas at 4 pm. Visited Golden Nugget, Four Queens, and Flamingo and spent about an hour and a half. MGM Grand Hotel is very magnificent." The family drove through the night sleeping in the car. Sometime in the middle of the night, the boys wake up the smooth road had turned into a dirt road.

"Thursday, July 4, 1974, slept in car Dusty Winding Rd., Cedar City Utah lost the muffler on a Rocky detour." After driving 4388.6 miles with still 2000 miles from home, the interstate highway roads stopped. The map of the United States in McClary school wasn't entirely accurate. The Eisenhower interstate highway system wasn't complete in 1974. A dirt road detour for about 50 miles was ahead of the family. Still, the father's skills managed to get the family to the Sandman hotel in Grand Junction, Colorado. Leaving Utah and the AMC ambassador's muffler behind.

"Friday, July 5, 1974, had a good night's rest that hotel left about 10 am heading to Denver. Had picnic lunch in the Rockies, stopped at Stuckey's light supper drove through the night. "At one point, Kansas highway patrol stopped the father and, after a lengthy discussion, allowed the family to continue on their way with a warning about driving a car with no muffler. The father embarked on the most extended driving length of the trip to this point. He had driven four times through the night. With the intensity and concentration of Monet painting water lilies, he goes 1131.8 miles in 36 hours. He will be so focused he needs a navigator through the night, which the older children will take turns doing.

"We're close to Kansas City on Saturday, July 6, 1974, at 10:07 am. Stopped at McKenzie's restaurant for breakfast called sisters in Iowa, stopped for gas at St. Louis, headed for Indianapolis for the night, arrived at the Ramada Inn at 10:30 pm".

"Sunday, July 7, 1974; went to church at Saint Michael's, Greenfield, Indiana 10;30 mass. On the road again at 12:35, dinner at Nicholson's restaurant, arrive back home in Amsterdam, New York, at 7:30 pm." At this point, the mother stops writing, and the diary ends. The family traveled 6,251.4 miles and spent $1,177.93 in fifteen days. The road trip ended with a new perception. And a way of looking at the house on Ellsworth Street with fresh eyes. The father resells the trailer and will eventually trade the AMC ambassador for a Chrysler Town and country with air conditioning. In 1992 the Eisenhower interstate highway system will officially be complete. Including that stretch of 50 miles in Utah. The Ellsworth Street boys get a new family dog, another shepherd named Brutus. It's one thing to be in a country, to say I'm from this land because I know this area, but never going any further. It's different to see a country, mile by mile, to know that America is more than what a person says. You can't learn about this in a book. You must go out and find it Travel does broaden the mind.

"Top cross-section"

You son, yes you, I'm talking to you. I'm a proud official member of the BSA. To describe myself, I'm Two hollow aluminum tubes 3/4 of an inch in diameter long, curved at a slight 20° angle and approximately 11 inches, forming the letter C. In the center, there's a hole containing a Metal grommet connecting two parts, creating the letter X if you're looking from the top down. I am the top cross-section of an official Boy Scout Tent from 1969. I'm strong. I'm made at temperatures over 2000 degrees, unlike these flimsy plastic tent polls they make today from China! I'm made in the USA, and proud, I was assigned to the Boy Scout troop 26 of the Sir Willian Johnson Counsel in 1969. Our troop had six patrols Beaver Bobcat, Bear, Wolf, Fox, and Elk. On my honor, I will do my best to do my duty to God in my country and to obey the scout law to always help other people to keep myself physically strong, mentally awake, and morally straight. That's the boy scout pledge, which along with the pledge of allegiance, was said by every scout at every scout meeting in Woodrow Wilson elementary school.

Service is the rent we pay for our space on earth, and the proud 26th were truly capable of giving service. In the first two years, my troop was a beehive of activity. The Scoutmaster, his son, and his other friends would go winter hiking, climb Mount Marcy, summer canoeing on the chain lakes along with the spring camporee at Sans Souci, the fall at Arch George, the summer camp out at Woodworth Lake, and of course Scout Island on the great Sacandaga lake.

Those first few years seemed to go by in a mad rush as the Scoutmaster worked with his son on the merit badges to become an Eagle Scout. In the spring of 1971, the Scoutmaster's son made eagle, and there was a picture in the paper. My fellow boy scout tents were very proud of the son. Of course, achieving Eagle means the end of their scout career. He and his friends were leaving the scout troop. The Scoutmaster planned on one more adventure hike to the high desert of New Mexico. Philmont Scout ranch. I wasn't with him that summer; I was assigned to the rest of the troop at Woodworth Lake. All I know is what was in the papers, there was an accident in which the Scoutmaster died. On that summer evening, there was a memorial eulogy done in his honor at the Woodworth Lake campsite.

 Tragedy affects different people in different ways, and the new Scoutmaster who took over the troop seemed to have been affected by the tragedy. The council had planned to recruit 500 new Boy Scouts. It was during this time I met the two brothers. They were encouraged to join scouting and came to their first meeting at the school. They had no uniforms, no scout handbook, but liked camping and wanted to be part of the troop.

Soon the meetings turned into a routine, after the boy scout pledge, the new scoutmaster would just drink beer and play cards with his friends, and the boy's played dodgeball in the gym. No one worked on merit badges at all. Soon the assistant council leader would be at more and more meetings. Only once did the new scoutmaster have the boys work on a merit badge that was for first aid and took the boys to the volunteer ambulance company.

The two Brothers wanted to work on merit badges, one decided to try to get a journalism merit badge, they found an old mimeograph printer in the basement of their Ellsworth Street house. and they tried to make a newspaper of course they failed no Scoutmaster offered advice or instructions. "You have to go to the summer camp to get any badges," the scoutmaster said. The brothers couldn't afford to go, but the Boy Scouts did offer a program which is to sell door-to-door Burpee seeds. I know what you're going to say "girl scouts have delicious cookies. Boy scouts had Seeds!" so in the spring the brothers went door-to-door trying to raise enough money but failed so they never went to the summer camp

With no uniforms and no assistance for merit badges, the brothers went to the spring camporee at Sans Souci, lake pleasant where there was a great big sand dune was jump down on it was fun. Second campout fall camporee at Arch George was also fun, but I noticed the patrols had no leaders and soon no guidance. It was up to me, Top cross-section, to keep strong for the sake of the scouts.

The third campout was for the polar bear patch at Arch George, this was going to be a winter campout. The expected high temperature was -4 below. The boys who stayed for the weekend would receive the polar bear patch. The patch is given to camping out in subzero weather, so you really have to be prepared. When the brothers first arrived, other boys got into a big snowball fight, the two brothers didn't, they focused on getting their tent set up and finding firewood. It turns out the boys who got in a snowball fight got wet and they had to be sent home. In zero weather if you get wet, you'll freeze and you cannot stay warm. Life below zero is a battle it's a war we have to constantly fight it all the time make sure you don't sweat make sure you don't burn yourself because if your putting your hands too near the fires you'll also burn yourself without knowing it. Many did this too, which is ironic saying that it's -4° outside but go home with a burn. There were several teams of ambulances right there that spent the night in case boys couldn't make it. The brothers didn't need any assistance they slept in the tent. It was so cold wrapped up into sleeping bags and long johns . You dressed and undressed inside the sleeping bag.

There is something about the cold about being in the cold for two days and nights that forces you to focus on yourself and survival. Like the way aluminum tent polls are made in, it will temper your resolve, and make boys strong. At the end, of the 35 Boy Scouts of Troop 26, only 7 got the polar bear patch the two brothers were among them they accomplished something. their father picked them up from camp, the replacement scoutmaster went home early as well. I was their cross-section BSA tent and I was with them. Because the leaders went home early, I was wrapped up and put in the fathers truck. I was then placed in the attic of a house on Ellsworth St until the spring. That spring boy Scout troop 26 was officially disbanded, and I remained in the attic until a few years later the brothers just went camping with their dad and I was put to service again. The family used us for camping and hiking many times And although I was considered heavy and bulky I was solid and strong as I was

BSA created. The two brothers had two other brothers the youngest got to be an Eagle Scout.

BSA's Sir Willian Johnson Counsel was dissolved, and all the property was sold off. I think of all those young boys, instead of camping are now taking Ritalin and becoming school shooters.

The top cross-section is substantial and connects both sides of boys to help them to become men. Even when led by a scoutmaster who's lost his sense of Direction, they cannot do much damage to boys because a strong top cross-section gives you support when the leaders have failed. During your life, you will have many crossroads. Having a proper Top cross-section makes all the difference.

"1000 small miracles".

"Please remember the ghost light as you enter the stage," that is the sign on the stage door. The third sister saw that sign as they closed the door for the last time. They had finished striking the set of the previous children's show at the high school. "I'll call you tonight, "her friend said as she left to go home. Tomorrow was Thanksgiving, and there was that frosty trace of snow on the ground that you smell and feel in late November, with winter just around the corner. The third Sister had a small part in the show and helped backstage. The High School principal directed "Pinocchio," and he managed to get every elementary school student into the high school for all three shows. The next show will be a spring Musical. These weren't just high school shows; he got union musicians to play, which is why "Fiddler on the Roof" and "Hello Dolly" sounded so good in the small town of Amsterdam, N.Y. Her friend called as soon as she got home, there was another show going on and he asked her if she wanted to be in it. The third sister started her Senior year of high school wearing a Bowler hat, had visions of Liza Minnelli, and would listen to the Movie soundtrack of Cabaret on the record player; she'd play the record repeatedly until the grooves ran thin. But in a moment of channeling, Judy Garland blurted out, "let's put on a show," to her friends on the phone. They were talking about a Christmas show that would be canceled unless they got more actors. It's the second time this show was going to be canceled. The first time was when the music teacher unexpectedly departed.

The Christmas show was a small student run theater group called YPPA, which stands for (young people for the performing arts). It existed from December 8, 1971, to December 16, 1972. During that time, the group performed; "You're a good man Charlie Brown," "Animal Farm," "Our Town," "leaves of grass," "Hill Farm," "Summertree," "Christmas Carol," and "Gift of the Magi."

The High School principal, who had just finished directing the children's show at the high school, was still running Man of La Mancha and didn't have time to assist with the YPPA Christmas show. So, there was no teacher supervision. The school board was going to cancel the last YPPA show. "We need publicity, sets, costumes, props, lighting and actors, lots and lots of actors." let's go to the principal's office and ask him," the third sister said. Although young, the third Sister had moments of fearlessness and tenacity of a jack Russell terrier who once got a taste of a good thing and would not let it go. The following Monday, the third sister and her theater friends approached the high school principal. "We can do this show. Just give us a chance," she said to their Principal with a look of steel-eyed resolution and determination. The Principal saw the decision on their faces and agreed to let them try. The kids had their performance, but now they had to make it happen.

The Christmas carol /Gift of the Magi was three weeks away, so there wasn't much time. After school, she walked through the house up to her room. She noticed her two younger brothers playing with dinosaurs. "Do you want to be in a play?" she said to them The brothers had no idea what she was talking about but always had that politeness about them and would always answer yes, regardless of what she said. So, she found two new cast members, a ten-year-old and an eight-year-old who were now going to be Cratchit brothers, in a Christmas Carol.

The Actor on stage is only 10% of the production. The other 90% is like an iceberg and lies below the water. The public never sees that 90%. The purpose is for the audience never to notice that part; if they do, the cast has failed. The purpose of theater is to create that illusion to take you away to another space. This is what that music teacher taught the friends of the third sister. And she, for her part, also discovered that theater wasn't something to be afraid of, That Theatre is an excellent place to learn inspiration and confidence. With two weeks to go, they finally got a cast together. They must still find some costumes, and props, build a set, and find lighting. Rehearsals were at the First Presbyterian Church, and the student director met her entire cast for the first time. Getting 24 people together in one room for anything, much less a December Christmas play, is an arduous task, which they somehow did. After Thanksgiving, the third sister brought her two brothers to three rehearsals. They were part of the Cratchit family. The older of the two brothers had one line in the play. The third sister was in both plays as the ghost of Christmas past and the second show, "Gift of the magi," as the sympathetic next-door neighbor. We must find Costumes, old pants, and clothes so the brothers look poor like a Cratchit family should look.

The cast was ready for opening night with a dress rehearsal in the rear-view mirror. Of course, dress rehearsal means 1000 things to do, 1000 props to get, 1000 lights to focus on, 1000 sets to finish, 1000 costumes to adjust, and you're running on adrenaline, coffee, and high expectations. The student Director, constantly bombarded by questions, managed to keep her cast together, "Work as an Ensemble" is what the music teacher told them to do. The ensemble is a French word that means working together. Going on stage the first time is an exhilarating rush, lights are so bright, you can't see anything except the other actors. It was terrifying and exciting at the same time but perfect for the third sisters theatrical training. The weather forecast predicted some snow, about 6 inches, not enough to cancel the show, but enough to make it interesting. The piano accompanist who was to be playing music from the recent Broadway musical Scrooge did not show up, so the cast sang the songs Acappella.

Still, it was well received and had an excellent small audience. The Saturday night show again went very well. The school principal was there. This was the last show the YPPA performed at the Clara bacon elementary school amphitheater. Because of a snowstorm, the final performance was canceled. Still, 6 inches of snow in upstate New York isn't a reason to cancel the show. It's just an inconvenience. The third sister's theater friends didn't know this then, but the piano accompanist came down with the flu. Still, it was a good show, and all are actors who were in it should be proud. They were trying to put on a show to entertain, just trying to do with the music teacher told them to do. "Work as an ensemble" is a good lesson for doing a show and for many life events you'll have in the future. It was a good show, and the YPPA was proud to be part of the third sister's education and theatrical training. She went on to have a significant role in the spring musical. After graduation, her theater friends went their separate ways. Some did more theater, some did not. As she closed the door of the elementary school amphitheater, snow was falling, winter had begun, and she had a feeling of accomplishment. Being a part of a meaningful theatrical event that she worked on to create was good.

"Watchers of the wall."

Adventures of Brutus and Visker toddler.

To the rest of the world, he looked fierce. If you walked on his territory unwelcomed, he could tear your lungs out with one bite. To the kids at Ellsworth Street, he was just the dog, Brutus. They got them young, maybe a one-year-old pup. At the same time, they also got a young kitten named Visker toddler. The German Shepherd and the little cat instantly bonded and slept together in the doghouse. The retaining wall well defined the property. That stretched the length of the property on Clizbe and Ellsworth. "Stop, advance and give the countersign," Brutus would say. Of course, humans can't understand dog talk, so all they heard was a series of barks. But the barks were ferocious enough for people to stop. Brutus had to smell you; if you were a friend, you could pass. Oh, by the way, he always knew who the friends were. Viskar Toddler could also communicate in dog talk. After all, she was a brilliant cat. As Brutus stuck strictly to the wall and the perimeter, Visker would go on Recon across the Street and down to the pond where there were many fish and birds. Coming back to the doghouse, she'd report vital information about squirrel activity and chipmunk gatherings to Brutus.

The only serious threat to the guards of the wall was the blue man. The man in the blue suit with a blue bag seems to come and go as he pleases and puts letters in a black box. He refused to give the countersign despite Brutus repeatedly telling him to do that. Visker would prowl the neighborhoods, find out where the Blue Man was, and report back to the doghouse. One day the humans forgot to put Brutus on the chain leash and found out Blue Man was coming. Brutus sat in the doghouse, waiting for his chance. Suddenly the Blue Man went down the Street on the other side of the wall. Brutus decided to advance to the edge of the wall, giving his barks. The Blue Man stopped but did not cross. Brutus, would not cross the wall, staying on his side of the wall, so a Mexican standoff began

 "This is interesting," Visker said. "What's going on now?"

"Well, as long as he doesn't cross the wall, I can't smell him," Brutus responded. "Well, what do you want me to do," Visker said. "I can't stand around here all day. I've got birds and chipmunks to watch." Brutus was showing his teeth, which were very white and very large. "I'll try to approach the Blue Man," Visker said. "He doesn't look very dangerous to me." "All right, just be careful," Brutus responded. Visker walked up to the Blue Man, and he responded by petting her. Brutus saw this as an act of respect, so he stopped barking and backed down, "Ok blue man, you can advance for now," Brutus said, "but we'll be watching you carefully."

Open House Baseball

Roger Maris was traded to the Saint Louis Cardinals in 1967, so the New York Yankees weren't the same again. He thought of this as he closed his locker for the last time on the last day of the last class of his senior year of high school.

His team would be quite different from the Yanks of "61" and "62", The team he grew up with, that legacy team of the 50s that seemed to win a World Series every year was slowly changing. They lost the World Series in 1964 and getting older. The first brother is getting older but will always play Baseball and follow his Yanks. With the winter snow melted away to expose the spring grass of his baseball field on Ellsworth Street, those familiar feelings of Yankees and younger days stir once more. He thought we would play Baseball one more time on the baseball field. After all, it was his field and graduation party; if he were old enough to be drafted into Vietnam, he would certainly do what he pleased. He made his Field of Dreams, and nobody else but his friends could play there.

  The summer of 1967 on Ellsworth Street started with a graduation party and a baseball game. There's a photograph of the first brother standing there, hands up in jubilation, while friends look on in the background, drinking beer. The picture had gotten such notoriety of family lore that each of his younger brothers tried to imitate the photograph of him standing, hands up in triumphant jubilation, with gleeful confidence at a job done, a mission completed. It's a photograph that has been re-staged repeatedly; it's that feeling of high school graduation in 1967. The media concocted an idea for calling it the summer of love, but that term was just invented to sell records and newspaper articles. In reality, the summer of 1967 was the summer of the Open House baseball game Graduation Party of Ellsworth Street.

The Ellsworth Street House looked a little different in 1967. the house was white, and there were more trees as Dutch elm disease hadn't taken its toll yet. There were several lilac bushes, and the old concrete retaining wall remained intact. There was no garage, making the baseball field yard was larger. The driveway that went around the house was dirt and gravel. Home plate was next to the lilac bush at the top of the driveway facing Ellsworth the first base line went North to Rezneak's yard, the second base went to the boundary of the Kryzacks and Morello house; third base lay behind the oak tree.

His high school graduation in 1967 was warm but humid, one of those days that waits for a graduation party like this, with cold winters forgotten and the inconsistencies of spring giving way to burst out of life everywhere, becoming proper summer. The first brother was the first one to graduate in his generation, so everyone was there. They were grandparents, aunts, uncles, cousins, relatives who came from far away, neighbors, and friends. The father put a big sign saying "open house" at the corner with a banner stretching from one end of the property to the next. There needed to be more outdoor lawn chairs. The kitchen was a buzz of activity and drinks, and sandwiches were prepared. Hamburgers had to be cooked outside on the father's grill. More chairs from the house were put out as well. "Open House" is a term used to describe a house selling, but today it's a special meaning because today, there will be a huge graduation party and an even greater Baseball game.

The father bought kegs of beer. The first brother's friends drink had had a good time. The grandfather sat on the chair underneath the Apple tree, whose buds just started to come out. Drafted in 1917, he went off to fight in a war to end all wars. Setting up the charcoal on the fireplace that he built to cook burgers, the father, after his own graduation, joined the Navy in 1940 to fight the second war to end all wars. These men knew combat and wanted their son and grandson to have nothing to do with it. After all, this is what they fought for, to live in peace, but today was not that day. It was not the day for negative thinking. It was a day of celebrations and backyard baseball.

Maybe it was the combination of beer on a hot summer day and the fact that his friends and family were having fun one more time on this field that they enjoyed so many times that first brother and his friends playing Wiffle Ball on their ball field became their heroes of past Yankee teams. So instead of the first brother and his friends playing on their field, they were playing with the "61" Yankees. The party was watching Yogi Berra, Don Larsen, Mickey Mantle, and Roger Maris play Baseball in the backyard of Ellsworth Street or, to be more precise. Forty-two degrees, fifty-seven minutes, nineteen seconds, North b. By seventy-four degrees, t. Ten minutes and twenty-four seconds west of the prime Meridian. This was the location of his home plate, the baseball field, the And the Whiffle Ball game, and the old Yankee Stadium for one summer graduation day. The father, the grandfather, and all the younger brothers and family members were in the stands.

Baseball's one of those fine summer sports where you can sit back and relax and watch, no television, no music necessary, it's a sport for backyard summer graduation parties. The first brother started the game with the ball connected to deep right field, almost going to Rezneak's yard for and making it into a double. Yogi Berra hit a line drive to score the first run. The next batter hits a high line drive only to be caught by a leaping grab from Mickey Mantle. The ball field is smaller than when First brother and his friends first played on it ten years ago. They had gotten bigger and taller. The wiffleball in the backyard will not carry like a baseball.

But with two men on and two outs in the bottom of the ninth, the baseball game took a serious tone. It's time to bring in Don Larsen. Larsen approaches the mound, the only man to throw a complete game no-hitter in a World Series. The batter comes to the plate, with the first pitch a screaming fastball, and the batter swings. Ice cream pops. Larsen does his wind-up second pitch. The crowd sits on the edge of their seat, the younger brothers waiting in anticipation, dropping down their sodas. A swing and a miss, strike two. Everyone at the graduation party stops what they're doing and looks at this. This is the last strike to the final out. Can they, do it? Can they win the game?

Memory is an uncertain thing. Still determining if it was a miss or If they finally got to Larsen in the end, but all we know is it's a memorable first high school graduation party.

"Northampton shop"

A 1972 forest-green Oldsmobile Cutlass drives North along Route 30 to the great Sacandaga lake. The car belonged to her grandfather recently departed. The first sister has her apartment in Massachusetts, where a white cat waits for her. Like the first sister, the cat enjoys travel and each other's company. They value independence. To achieve this, she works for three different newspapers and also a part-time job at a pharmacy to afford a tiny little apartment. The apartment is in a converted barn on the border of Massachusetts and Rhode Island near Fall River. But it makes her independent, and independence is a gift. The first sister, like the grandfather, looked at the struggle of self-reliance as a virtue, not a handicap. Today she is driving up to meet the rest of the family at the summer camp. A Boston Globe press pass is attached to her purse; she is, at last, her own person.

  She started her drive in the late morning. It was one of those beautiful mornings in upstate New York. In high summer, trees are green against a cobalt blue sky with low humidity and little puffs of clouds floating by from the west. Route 30 heads due north, and after passing the village of Broadalbin, the Adirondack mountains open in a vista before her. It's a picture of a perfect drive on a perfect day that you would see on a cover of a travel brochure. A day that only occurs once or twice and always in late July or early August. As she talks to her passenger, one of the younger brothers more interested in swimming in the lake and being in the boat, she gets a picture of the perfectness of her surroundings. Working as a reporter, she is always looking for a story, and because ideas come from local papers, she wants to get a newspaper.

As she passes the town of Northampton, she starts looking for a shop or store. At last, she sees what looks like an old barn at first, but as she drives closer, she sees the sign that says open. "let's stop here; I want to get a newspaper," she says to the brother as she pulls the car into a gravel driveway. Around the property on the front of the business is various farming equipment rusting in the sun. A wagon wheel, an old-fashioned plow, the remains of a 1930s Model T, and a sign that says, "General store." The term a general store in Northern New York can and almost does mean everything and anything the proprietor would want it to mean.

Some of the outside "antiques" had been there so long small trees were starting to pop up. Along with a combination of antiques, some real, some imaginary, was a collection of various eclectic items whose actual purpose is known by the locals living in the vicinity. From firewood, Swiss army knives, camping gear, seeds, fishing lures, Live bait, Shotgun shells, animal traps, warm woolen mittens, Snowshoes, Binoculars, socks, Cans of Sterno, sweet corn, inflatable floats, postcards and stamps, ice cream, clothing, and perhaps newspapers.

 The first sister stopped and parked the car. It was, in fact, the only car in the parking lot. She pushed an old screen door with a bell on the top that made that tiny ring as she entered. The younger brother followed behind. At first, there was no one in the shop. So, she walked around looking at the various items for a few minutes, old military uniforms, paint-by-number kits, kites, hand-woven baskets, cap guns, and a stand that said newspapers but was empty. "I'm so sorry I was in the back," the storekeeper said, appearing through an old doorway with animal traps dangling from the sides, wiping her hands with a towel. "I was just in the middle of making strawberry preserves. Do you like strawberry preserves?"

The storekeeper was a lady in her early 60s. She had the look of a person who worked hard all her life. Hands were worn, and she wore the dress and apron of a 1950s housewife, with a warm, friendly face in her horned-rimmed glasses looked at first sister and said, "May I help you"? The first sister had the feeling that she was the first and only customer she's had all day and replied, "do you have any newspapers"? "No, we sold the last Leader-Harold this morning, and we don't get the gazette up here," the storekeeper responded, seeing no other newspapers and not wanting to embarrass her by asking her if she had the New York Post or Daily News. The first sister politely replied. "Oh, thank you, I'll just look around." The storekeeper watched the Sister for a few minutes. The Boston Globe Press pass dangled from her purse and caught the eye of the storekeeper, "are you a reporter"? Well, yes, I am," the first sister responded. The mood of this storekeeper changed from that friendly Northern New York, "Hi, neighbor, just passing by," to the over-excitement as if she had too many cups of coffee. "I've got lots of stories here," she said. "Do you want to hear a good story" the storekeeper began talking as if hooked up to an adrenaline pump. "I want to tell you all about these stories. I have a lot of stories", Soon, the storekeeper told the first sister about her entire life. She couldn't stop talking, and the first sister, being polite, didn't want to interrupt. Soon the first sister was sitting with the storekeeper, having a cup of coffee. The storekeeper showed her all sorts of craft ideas, scraps of newspaper clippings, photographs of her husband, recently departed, and all these plans she had for her business.

There was the story about her husband, who worked for 30 years logging and died of a heart attack when he retired and never collected Social Security. Then a son went to California to study something that she forgot about, and then there was the farm that was once a dairy farm but closed, so she tried to repurpose it into an antique store. Then the escaped prisoner and the friend of the uncle's brothers, the cousin's nephew, who thinks he saw him in the woods. Then there was the time of the big car crash on Route 30 that almost killed the man. Then there was the time about the lost teenager in the woods, and then there was the time. The stories kept going on about this. The first sister seemed unable to get a word in edgewise. She wasn't that kind of reporter. She reported on human interest stories, scrimshaw, basket weaving, and soap box Derby races. She did, however, report on selectman and council member's meetings at town halls and school board meetings which were bread and butter to a reporter, a way to make a daily living but not something of any interest. Even the fishing Derby they held in February seemed interesting, but she wasn't a fishing person. To be a good reporter, one must look for a story objectively and not be part of the story. But this trend had been more prevalent since she first started going to the field of newspaper reporting. She saw more and more and was evidently on display with the little storekeeper in upstate New York. Storekeepers' ideas for stories were not the story, the story, Is the reporter or the first sister reporting the story. After about one hour, the first sister looked over at her younger brother, who was fidgeting and looking outside the window. He wanted to get going to the camp. "These are all very interesting 'she said to the storekeeper, "give me your phone number, and I'll call you later, "the storekeeper complied, and finally, they returned to the car and returned to the summer camp.

Back in the car, the first sister felt uneasy, and she didn't like to be the story. She felt the need to be objective, but the storekeeper pushed her to be subjective. Subjectivity was a trend; more and more, other reporters were lapping this up like a dog laps up water on a hot day. The first sister's desire to seek facts, even in a human-interest story, ended with a lonely shopkeeper seeking attention. People like the storekeeper have been putting newspaper reporters on a higher standard, almost revering them as if they're on Mount Olympus and everyone else is somehow a child of a lesser God. The first sister didn't like that feeling. She believed the important thing was for the reporter to be anonymous.

Huntersland

At 4:30 in the morning, they come to the cafe in the Middleburg for the hunter's breakfast. Some are old, some middle age and some are very young. They tell their hunting stories. They are telling stories about hunting the bear, the deer, the geese of the pheasant. They talk about guns, shotguns, rifles, crossbows, and muskets, all hunting stories. Every hunter, there's a story, and the young boys are here, too. They are listening and learning. They're here to learn, here to become men. Becoming a man is an art form. It is also challenging to become a man, but it starts with the hunt. To hunt, you went back into the woods 24,000 years ago. Cave paintings in southern France. Of mastodons and woolly mammoths and the men who hunted them, it hasn't changed. It never changes—stories of grandfathers and hunting trips, the first stories that turned into cave paintings. About the incredible animals, they sought.

Some of the stories are real, some are bits and pieces with fiction thrown in for good measure, but all are the same stories they've been telling forever. Right before dawn, they walk up the hills in darkness, crunching snow on freshly frozen old leaves, the only sounds. The constellation of Orion has shifted to the southeast. All that is here is what you have. No cell phone service is available. Everything you bring in; you must also bring out because you take care of the land. The mountain is forever, and we are temporary. The land is always carefully tended to by the hunter. Anything carried in is always taken out, for the hunter knows the mountain is forever, and we are all passersby.

The old Schoolhouse is at the foot of the mountain. The sign says built-in 1813. going up the Hill, the hunter passes the old stone walls built long ago; they go up through the mountain fields. Even apple orchards sit there rotting away. Slowly the sun is making the sky brighter at the mountaintop. And the top of the Hill? But in the bottom with the hunter sets, it is still dark. There are still a few more minutes to go. Sitting there, he remembers his hunting years past. When he was standing right by a tree, seen three doe passes by so close he could hear their breath. He didn't move. His hand wasn't on the gun. The act of moving to take the gun up scared the doe away. So, he watched them pass by in the early morning light. But that isn't this morning. This morning, the Schoolhouse is closed, and education starts.

"Home for Christmas"

Wednesday, December 22. 9:30 pm the night before Christmas Eve, the youngest brothers go to bed after watching Rudolph the Red-Nosed reindeer and frosty the snowman on network television. The first sister and first brother stay up late and discuss Christmas presents and shopping. They'll go to Main Street tomorrow afternoon To Woolworths or Grants department store. The Christmas tree has already been brought inside but not decorated. They'll do that tomorrow; they will get the boxes in the attic filled with Christmas decorations from years past, Some hand made in kindergarten at McCleary elementary school. But they'll wait and put them up. They'll go to school tomorrow morning, the last day of classes before the Christmas holiday and Santa Clause.

A bus Departs Ames, Iowa 10:20 pm; The Second Sister is on this bus with her ticket in hand, which she passes to the driver, who will rip off half and hand her the rest. She is traveling from Ames, Iowa, to Davenport, Iowa. Chicago, Illinois. South Bend, Indiana. Cleveland, Ohio, Pittsburgh, Pennsylvania. New York City, and finally home to Amsterdam, New York. This trip home will take her thirty-seven hours, just in time for the Christmas holiday and Christmas eve dinner. She thinks of the rest of the family, the brothers and sisters putting up the Christmas tree. And wonders if the father bought it at Bob's trees, where at a discount price of $3, you could walk into the woods and find a tree and cut it down yourself.

Thursday. December 23. The bus arrives in Davenport, Iowa 1:22 am. The sudden stopping of a bus movement wakes up the second sister. They must change buses here to go to Chicago, so she takes her luggage with her as she goes into the empty bus terminal, except for the few travelers traveling late at night. The cold winter air and clear sky remind her of snow and past Christmases. She hopes they'll be snow for Christmas. It had snowed a week before, about 6 inches, so there is snow on the ground, but the sky is still clear. The House on Ellsworth Street is silent, everyone sleeping. News reports say there's a chance for snow on Christmas Day.

The bus departs Davenport, Iowa 2:25 am, and back on the Interstate, she falls back to sleep again. Moving through the Illinois Prairie, the Stars are out. Smoke rises from the kitchen chimney of Ellsworth Street at 4:35 am. The two middle brothers come outside and wait for the van to drop off the Gazette newspapers. The house has two fireplaces and a wood-burning stove. Their task before they deliver newspapers is to light the kitchen stove fire so the kitchen is warm for the morning.

Just before five O'clock in the morning, the Schenectady gazette van stops and drops off their newspapers at the corner of Ellsworth Street in Clizbe Avenue. They have 200 newspapers to deliver in the morning on a newspaper route inherited from their older brother even their sisters delivered newspapers.

The bus arrives in Chicago, Illinois 5:35 am. The second sister gets out to transfer to another bus again. This time, the bus terminal is a little more crowded as people are moving by getting ready for the morning. In Chicago, Christmas wreaths are everywhere, the sign of the seasons. The two middle brothers get home from delivering the papers in the morning. The kitchen is warm now. Slowly the house comes to life. The mother wakes up and gets ready for her workday. She drives to Albany thirty miles each way and works for the state of New York. The father gets up, starts up, and warms up the engine of her Toyota Corolla. He'll also start the engine of the Chevy truck he drives to work at the Scotia naval depot. He's got his football pools in for the weekend games. The third sister and the two youngest brothers get up and get ready for the school day. It's the last day of classes before the Christmas holidays, and the breakfast talk is about presents. Who's been nice and naughty, and will Santa Claus come this year? The mother talks about the second daughter on her way home, hopefully arriving safely.

Grandmother comes in right before Mother leaves for work. She's watching the youngest brother, who doesn't go to school yet, as the two brothers go to McClary Elementary. Another brother goes to middle school, and the third sister goes to high school and takes off. The grandmother will sit and prepare the Kucious, or the traditional Lithuanian Christmas Eve dinner.

At 10:30 am, the Second sister's bus Departs Chicago, Illinois. It's a cold morning. She sees smoke rising from chimneys everywhere. As the bus slowly leaves urban areas and goes back into the vast expanses of Indiana Prairie land, she thinks about her own home and Christmas.

At McClary Elementary school, the fourth brother is finishing his Christmas decoration he's doing. He will place this on the Christmas tree tonight when they finish the decorating. The third brother listens to other friends talking about Santa Claus and which track he'll take in class. And when he goes and leaves the North Pole, they're apprehensive about this as the weather might get nasty.

At 7:35 pm, The second sister's bus arrives in Cleveland, Ohio, where she'll transfer again. It's good to get off and stretch your legs before walking into another terminal filled with holiday travelers, students going home, and people returning to loved ones. Back at Ellsworth Street, the Third sister and the four brothers have finished setting up the Christmas decorations and tree. They put their wreath with Santa Claus on the doorway outside. They put on the outdoor and indoor lights. They put tinsel and Garland everywhere. Christmas bells hang suspended by the ribbon on top of the threshold between the dining and living rooms. All the boxes from the attic are empty. The house looks festive, and everyone's getting in the Christmas Spirit.

The third sister will drive the three youngest brothers to Saint Casimir's Church and practice the midnight mass procession. They are altar boys, and the midnight mass procession is the most significant mass of the year. Father Balch has a rehearsal, so all practice to do their best.

The second sister departs Cleveland, OH, at 9:55 pm for another all-night bus ride. The sky is still clear and cold. The dry cold of the Prairie has been replaced by the damp chill of Lake Erie in the Great Lakes, and with that feeling, she knows she's getting closer to home and her own Christmas. Back at Ellsworth Street, her father watches the news. There's a chance of a storm coming from the South. But he thinks the second sister will miss the worst if She is home by Christmas Eve afternoon.

She arrives, In Pittsburgh, PA, at 11:00 pm. This time, she can transfer to another bus. A few more passengers get on. The same bus will be driving through the night to New York City. The bus driver takes a few more tickets from other people as they put their bags away, mainly students. And that bus departs Pittsburgh, Pennsylvania, at 11:53 pm.

December 24, Christmas eve, and the second sister's bus arrives in New York City, New York 7:35 am. The House on Ellsworth Street repeats the same tasks it did the previous morning. However, there is a visible excitement in the air tonight on Christmas Eve. The youngest brother reminds the father to put the light out. The special light is placed near the living room window to shine outside to guide Santa Claus, so he'll come to their house. The mother goes to work for half a day, but there will be an office Christmas party where she invites Annette to come over and visit. She's a coworker who lives alone and doesn't have a family. The father will work all day and ask the Wilsons to come over for the weekend. The opening of Christmas presents on Christmas Eve. Saint Casimir's midnight mass. And then relatives will come by, friends will visit, there will be snow at that Christmas, as there always is, and they'll go tobogganing at the Sanford farm. They'll return for another Christmas meal with their family on Christmas Day. The house on Ellsworth Street will be a beehive of activity. Tonight is the Kucios.

As the second sister departs New York City New York at 8:30 am, Grandmother and first sister work in the kitchen on the recipes for the traditional Lithuanian dishes. Grandmothers and mothers have prepared the Kugelis and all these Lithuanian dishes for generations. With her long journey finally over, the second sister steps off the bus in Amsterdam, NY, at 1:00 pm. The first sister will pick her up at the bus station downtown. The family on Ellsworth Street is complete. She will join her mother, grandmother, and other sisters in preparing the meal. She's made it home for Christmas.

----

73 Opel

The father of Ellsworth Street house had that skill. As his
children grew up and were of car-driving age, he purchased
a collection of used vehicles that he'd repair for his children.
The four brothers would watch as he used the oak tree in
the backyard to pull an engine out. The 57 Chevy, or was it a
62 Dodge, or the Impala convertible. They were a collection
of cars he'd work on. It is a known fact that children will
gravitate to a father when he is enjoying himself, and the
father's fascination with the workings of the internal
combustion engine was pure joy to watch.

Then there was a line of Opel's as well. Opel was a German/
French company that GM controlled. And GM imported
them. The engines were made in Germany, the bodies made
in France and assembled by GM. They were small, efficient,
and perfect for Ellsworth Street kids to learn how to drive.
There were three models of Opels in the United States, the
Kadett, the GT, and the Manta. Ellsworth Street would see
them all. There was the used brown Opal Kadett for the
second sister to drive across the country to Iowa. You could
see the road through the floorboards. But it was a good
running car that made many long-distance trips. Of course,
there was the Opel GT, which was called the poor man's
Camaro. Beautiful And sleek design with curved lines,
hidden headlights, and the five Speed stick shift 2-seater. It

was a beautiful car to see and watch, but as all beautiful things ended too quickly, the engine caught fire on Market Street.

The father purchased a used Opel Manta for $65. "Here, boys, you fix it and make it run, and I will register it. So, the brothers went to work on this car. First, the brothers removed the engine to replace the head gasket. Then the transmission is disassembled. The carburetor will be taken apart, and the gaskets will be replaced.

The exhaust manifold was followed by the starter, alternator, fuel pump, radiator, and battery cables, and when all this was done the boys relaxed and took a break. Next, the axels and brake line along with the bearings were replaced. Next, the boys took the gas tank apart to fix it, the rotors and tires were next. The rewiring of the entire electrical system followed them. At that point, the boys went to work on the car's interior. The car had one front seat, and was heavily rusted so Bondo was liberally applied. Finally, they painted the car black with an orange racing stripe.

It's very empowering to understand every part of a vehicle. The simple act of turning the key will complete the circuit, sending an electrical charge from the battery to a starter, making the starter rotate. That rotation will fire a spark plug to turn a crankshaft piston that would explode. Those simultaneous explosions would ignite other Pistons to explode at a certain time. Those Pistons exploding will be fed by fuel from a carburetor, which regulates the speed and power of an engine depending on how much fuel is used. That shifting a clutch, either manual or automatic, will signal to a transmission to move those baring's and tries to keep in motion until you decide to apply brake fluid to discs or drums on your wheels. The perpetual action of this perpetual motion that you build hand by hand and step by step and will be the result of your labor and work. The boys knew this machine, from the radiator to the exhaust manifold and muffler. The lights, wiring, interior paint job, it was all them and no one else. The boys knew this knowledge and had the confidence to face any machine in the future. Knowledge gained is a good investment for $65.

Finally, how it runs and goes down the road and back again. It was a used car, and it ran as best as used cars can. It did some trips, then stopped running, and life moved on. But I don't think the trips were important, as much as it was making the car work. making it work made it a part of yourself. This was the plan all along. Fathers don't live forever, but their knowledge of courage will, if you want to learn. And when you know cars, you have both knowledge and courage.

Runaway

It was a fun weekend; I can't forget that. Always hang on to the fun you have, because sometimes fun will come in short supply. So, on the bus, I would close my eyes and think of the weekend and weekends passed, parties, long drives to Woodstock, Ashokan Reservoir, talent shows, and bands playing out in the fields on Saturdays. My fantasy daydreams continued past Kingston and up I-90 to Albany, where I and other daydreams changed buses. That other world was occupied in the mind of a young girl sitting across the aisle from me. Her daydreams were filled with leprechauns, dancing Elvish Spirits and the celebration of spring. Being April 30th and on that calendar that other people may celebrate a Pagan Irish festival called Beltane. She was very young, probably 14- or 15-years old traveling alone. A thin blue coat that was too thin for the chilly night air of upstate New York in early spring. The young girl sitting alone with a very thin jacket got off the bus with me looking confused, lost even. Only the two of us got off the bus in Amsterdam, NY. It was about 7:30 at night. She approached me and said.

"Can you drive me to Watertown? I will live under the stairs, and I'll sweep and clean and I'll do whatever you want me to do."

I was startled as my constant daydream ended abruptly with the fact I was standing on a sidewalk ready to call my mother to pick me up from the bus station. But this silence lasted for a thousand years, but through these decades, I caught a long look of desperation on her face. At first, I thought I was dreaming and that this was just an extension of my long dream upon departing New Paltz. But I looked at her, and she looked at me, and there we were in Amsterdam, NY zip 12010, population 12000, I-87 exit off the thruway, people just didn't get stranded here.

"Pardon me?" I spoke.

"Well, if I can't stay at your house, will you drive me to Watertown?" she said.

"Watertown," I said. "Watertown is about 123 miles away, and I have no car."

Then the look of desperation turned into a nervous panic as her face turned into one sizeable violent equation she was trying desperately to solve. She looked for her helpful Daydream to comfort her, but the dancing leprechauns were nowhere to be found.

"I thought," she said, "I thought this town was closer."

Then she walked away toward an old man, the only other person on the street at that time of night probably drunk, probably coming from a Tavern. He was weaving and bobbing. Like most drunks do, I think I recognized him from the post office under "The Most Wanted" sign. Only one person was on the street other than this girl and me. I saw her begin talking to this man, and I thought this was not a safe place for her. So, I walked over to her and put my arm around her and said, "Come over here, dear, let's talk."

She instantly backed off me and gave me a look a caged leopard gives a zookeeper. The action had its desired effect, the other man backed off and started to walk away, and I felt better. There remained this young girl.

"Look," I said, "this is a dangerous place and not the place to get lost in."

At that point, an attitude shift was genuine yet unknown to me, for this was unlike anything I had ever experienced.

"I'll tell my mother I'm bringing home a friend from college, OK? "I called my house.

In a short time, she came with the car and me and Erica both got in, i told my mother this was a friend and that she had to spend the night.

"Friend," she said, "What kind of friend?"

My mother had various kinds of friends in her lexicon of English language interpretation. She liked John. There were quite respectable friends like John. There were loud friends like Kurt, whom she didn't like. Then there were GIRLFRIENDS.

Then the grilling began, "Is she a GIRLFRIEND? Why didn't she have enough money to get home?" This cross-examination lasted several hours, from when we got into the car to about two o'clock in the morning. I did my best. Before we were picked up at the station, I gave Erica a crash course on my life during four years of college at New Paltz. The lie was elaborate, with names, places, and actual classes. And Erica was an excellent liar.

The key aspects were missing, and my mother's analytical nature saw right through them. This girl was too young to go to college; she didn't know where Watertown was and would not tell us where she lived. I was too tired to keep up this lie and pleaded for the court's mercy.

"Mother, she is a runaway. I don't know where she is from, and I don't know where she will go tomorrow."

Mother was not surprised and relieved at the truth finally coming out. As to what to do next, we were still determining.

"Runaway? Runaways have no business in this house." She said.

The new battle began to keep Erica from being thrown out of the house.

She is just a young girl who needs help, a stranger in a strange land." I said.

"But she is a stranger. We know nothing about her. What if she murdered us in our beds, steals our china, what if, what if...."

She was running out of excuses, and I was running out of answers. So, we talked until fatigue overcame our fears and hopes for this strange girl who was our guest. At three a.m., we all retired.

The morning came as we had all hoped and dreaded it would. My mother awoke first and woke me up. I am a night person and hate to be woken up in the morning. My mother is a morning person who hates staying up late, so we were both tired.

I had to go to Radio School, and my mother drove to Albany to work. We both traveled together, and we decided to take Erica with us. Our house has three floors, and the attic is considered m room, but that night Erica slept there. I walked up quietly and slowly so as not to frighten her. I was at the foot of the bed and, in the slowest voice possible, said, "Erica," like a frightened deer, she jumped out of the bed as if she was acting in a horror movie, "we, my mother and I, are going to Albany. We could drop you off at the bus station."

"Drop me off in Schenectady. I have friends there."

Something about this girl made you feel sorry for her, maybe it was the fact that she was a total stranger in our house, or perhaps she was not running away from anything but running to something.

"I am going to Watertown to attend Beltaine," Erica said, "and there is a school there and everything. Maybe I could go to this school and live there."

Erica was right about one thing, not being liked at high school. There were so many ugly times in my high school career. I still feel the pain of it all. I, too, wanted to run away like Erica, live somewhere else, and hide from the world to protect my emotions from being ripped apart by cold people.

They needed someone different to pick on them and ridicule them. Pushed into a corner, I created a fantasy world where I was the center of attention; high school students need so much attention. Well, Erica was undoubtedly getting her share today. I sighed to myself as we drove to Schenectady to drop her off. She was reticent the entire time we spent in the car. She never told us her last name or who she knew in Schenectady. Nor did she say what to do with the one dollar my mother gave her. My mother told her about our problems and that a mother was worrying about her somewhere. Love is expressed differently. Erica was listening. She had a look on her face I had never seen before. Inside, the leprechauns danced, the world was safe and adventurous, and bad things happened to others, not her. I must have felt the same way because while she was showering, I slipped my name and number into her pocket, hoping for the best for her.

The Schenectady bus station arrived all too soon. Erica was about to get out of the car when my mother said, "Erica, I don

I know what you're like or what your mother is like, but I know how difficult things can get at home. Everything we do and go through will strengthen us in the long run. Just have faith in ourselves and trust in God."

With that, Erica exited the car, and I never saw her again.

It was two months later. We had planted the spring flowers and the garden was in bloom on a wonderful Saturday morning. I received a phone call.

"Hello, is this Stan?" the woman on the line said.

"Yes," I said, thinking this was another telephone vendor trying to sell me land in Florida or credit card insurance. "Who is this?"

"I'm Erica's mother. I got this phone number out of her pocket."

That night's past feelings and memories returned like a giant tidal wave of knowledge.

"Yes, I'm stan," I responded, "did she make it home alright?"

"Oh yes, tell me what happened." She spoke.

I told her the story of the strange girl who got off the bus with me in Amsterdam, the pagan Irish rituals, and the bus station in Schenectady. Erica's mother continued with a natural method of progressing a good story.

Erica called the mystery friend, and he was a professor at Union College. He, in turn, called a deputy sheriff who was a good friend and proceeded to pick up Erica at the bus station. He then called Erica's mom, who had been up all night, realizing that Erica was not in the mall, not at her friends', and not even in town. Somebody called the Amherst police and had been contacted about the same time Erica had come to our house. Erica's father, a professor, drove to Schenectady to pick up his daughter,

Now we can look back on Erica's adventure with delight, but it could have taken a sinister turn if she had encountered a different kind of person. On what would have otherwise been a sunny day, Erica chose to follow some leprechauns who probably gave her luck on that day.

Oh, good Shephard.

 He always chooses the furthest seat from the alter. Taking
out a prayer book, he flips through the pages. This was given
to him over half a century ago, and his youthful handwriting
is still visible on one of the pages - nearly illegible due to its
age. That's how he wrote his name when he was 10 years
old. He pulls out the mass cards, all received at funerals:
one for his father, mother, grandfather, and grandmother.
The four are arranged around a prayer book like an altar. For
each Mass he attends, he prays for his family as he lights a
candle. He doesn't stay through the whole thing - usually
leaving before communion - but sometimes he takes it too.
He focuses his thoughts on his ancestors. Closing his eyes,
he remembers the Lithuanian church in Amsterdam, NY, and
the many statues - purchased by a priest's sister over one
hundred years prior, brought from Italy or Lourdes, France

or London, England. With great care and effort, they were transported to their final resting place in America.

The memories of his upbringing are still imprinted in his mind: the grandfather teaching him how to act in an office, the grandmother not letting them go out until the snow melted and the temperature rose; the father showing him how to hunt and fish and fix car engines in a garage during winter; and the mother teaching him to be independent, to read and enjoy culture.

He had been sitting there, alone in the pews of the church, waiting for the sermon to begin. All he could think about were those young people wasting away hungover on a Sunday rather than going to church and believing in the Good Shepherd. He remembered one song from an old radio station by the Jefferson Airplane; it was about the shepherd and protecting his flock. Even though few of them showed up today, so long as there was someone here to pray to, the good things would never be forgotten but only the bad were insubstantial.

About the author.

Stan Strikolas has a learning disability since birth, which went undetected until he was 32. After flunking out of SUNY New Paltz in 1984, Stan kept his optimism and completed the course at the New School of Contemporary Radio. He also endeavored to have an artistic outlet. He was involved with music, theatre, made movies and wrote extensively short stories and poems. His last radio job was Radio Free America at WRPI. To make ends meet, Stan toiled away at minimum wage jobs throughout his life. His longest held position was as a home health aide over the past 30 years—a job that saw him through the COVID crisis and even brought him in contact with people in need of diagnosis. Now that technology allows it, Stan can share his voice and stories with you from upstate New York, where he is currently 62 years old. In fact, Kurt Vonnegut once made Stan coffee and told him he had stories to tell! If you'd like to get in touch with him, reach out.

Stanislav Strikolas facebook.com

Stan Strikolas Twitter @SStrikolas

edwardstanba@gmail.com

visit Stans blog.

lithuaniandreamtime.com

mail.

C&E Enterprises

PO Box G80

Wynantskill, New York

12198-9998

Made in the USA
Middletown, DE
02 July 2023

34240664R00031